D1207200

For you, me and everyone – S.P-H.

For Abi and James Charity – A.P.

First American Edition 2022
Kane Miller, A Division of EDC Publishing

Text copyright © Smriti Halls 2021
Illustrations copyright © Ali Pye 2021
Originally published in English by Farshore, now HarperCollinsPublishers Ltd, under the title:
Who Are You? Translated under licence from HarperCollins Publishers Ltd

All rights reserved. No part of this publication may be reproduced,
stored in a retrieval system, or transmitted, in any form, or by any means, electrical,
mechanical, photocopying, recording or otherwise without the prior written permission
of the publisher or a licence permitting restricted copying.

For information contact:
Kane Miller, A Division of EDC Publishing
5402 S 122nd E Ave, Tulsa, OK 74146
www.kanemiller.com
www.myubam.com

Library of Congress Control Number: 2021944902

Printed in Italy
1 2 3 4 5 6 7 8 9 10

ISBN: 978-1-68464-470-4

MIX
Paper from
responsible sources
FSC™ C007454

This book is produced from independently certified FSC™ paper
to ensure responsible forest management.

For more information visit: www.harpercollins.co.uk/green

WHO ARE YOU?

Smriti Halls & Ali Pye

Kane Miller
A DIVISION OF EDC PUBLISHING

How do you do!
Have you come far?

Who do you actually
think that you are?

What's going on?
What's this about?

Turn over the page,
we're going to find out!

*Dive into this book
and explore lots
of things that
make you
YOU!*

Look at your face, your ears, and your chin.
Now wiggle your nose and give a BIG grin!

Jiggle your eyes.
Are they twinkly and bright?

Little or
LARGE?

Are they dark?
Are they light?

Which eyes, ears, noses, chins, and smiles most look like yours?

It never stops growing,
your wonderful hair.

Is it tidy or neat?
Do you simply not care?

Is it *curly* or
STRAIGHT?

Is it **tied up** or free?

If it didn't get cut, how **long** would it be?

What do you like about your hair?

Who's in your family? Who's in your pack?

Who takes good care of you?
Who has your back?

Who makes you giggle?
Who hugs you tight?

Who reads your bedtime
story at night?

Who would you put in your picture?

When you're at home, what do you play . . .

Daring adventures in lands far away?
Perhaps you love books
or a favorite toy?

What are the games YOU really enjoy?

Spot all the things you love playing with!

Aunts and uncles,
grandpas and grans,

Who's in your BIGGER
family clan?

Cousins and godparents,
people you know,

Friends that you make
from the places you go.

Who else is important in your life?

On special occasions, do YOU look the part?
What do you wear when you want to look smart?

Do you look fancy? How are you dressed?
What do you wear when you're looking your best?

What would you like to wear to this party?

Where have you lived, and where have you been?
What have you visited? What have you seen?

The world is so big, but we always know,
There are new friends to meet wherever we go!

Can you name some of the places where you and your family and friends have lived or visited?

What do you see that's **delicious** to eat?

Salty or sour?
Spicy or sweet?

Foods of all sorts are
here on display . . .

What do you fancy eating today?

Can you find some of your favorite food?

Do you sing? Do you bounce? Do you skate, do you run?
There are a hundred and one DIFFERENT ways to have fun.

Do you read? Do you swim? Do you juggle or bike?
Keep looking around. What else do you like?

Would you like to join in with any of these activities?

Who's your mom's mom?
How far back can you go?

Who's your dad's dad?
How much do you know?

Where did they live?
What did they do?

A small part of THEM
is a small part of YOU!

Talk to the people in your family about their lives, especially older people. Ask them about THEIR parents and relatives too! You could make a family tree.

Your past and your present,
your sparkle, your smile,

Your likes and dislikes,
your hairdo, your style.

All of these things make YOU who YOU are.
You're completely unique!

YOU ARE A STAR!